Everyone has a story. Within all of us there is a complete and tangible comedy, drama, horror and adventure. We simply need to find a purpose and then be fearless enough to expose our dysfunctions, victories, wounds and dreams.

Her kisses are the sweetest I have ever known. When I think of her, my heart begins to beat faster. When I see her, there are colors around her that I am sure do not exist anywhere else in nature. I get near her and my fingertips pulse like a drum from the want of touching her soft, freckled skin and running my hands through her strawberry-blonde hair. The need to pull her close to me so that I can once again know the sultry pleasure of the taste of her lips and the feel of her velvet breath mingling with my own compels me to act willfully without consideration for any rules of convention or need for propriety. I want her badly with a persistence that seems to know no end.

This is a forbidden joy and in the resistance that I struggle to manage every day I find solace in the knowledge that she is mine. Madison loves me. She tells me every day. She shows me in the little things that she does to please me, in the way she is blatant in expressing her feelings about me publicly and her fierce shows of jealousy should anyone else show me any interest. We are not supposed to love each other because it isn't considered proper. She is a woman and so am I.

When I am with her, I never feel unwanted.

My mother is considered a gentle soul, cheerful and talented, beloved by all. My father left her before I was born and I have been her consequence ever since. They were the all-American couple, the dream team, the ones you read about in fancy magazines for local heroes who make good. For a time, their union showed promise. But the glitzy post in the big city architectural firm could not keep a string of posh pearls happy in the county-scene estate when there were jazz clubs competing with country clubs. And that was that.

Mother was quick to grow strong and stand on her own. She created a career that made her a legend in her own right. Somehow, I got lost in the shuffle. I was considered more problem than progeny and so I became known as a situation with which the family had to deal. They did not like me much and they told me every chance they got. I learned to stay very quiet at all times and keep my head in books. I came to believe that if I could just redeem myself in life, everything would be made good again. No matter how I tried, how many awards I won or trophies I brought home, it was just not enough to win their acceptance. Basically, I grew up in my room to the pleasure of all who actually knew of my existence.

When it comes to my family there is no illusion. I am unwanted.

Adam Campbell comes to my house every day now and has for over a month for the sole purpose of asking me to go out with him on a date. Surely, this is too long for someone to operate under the misapprehension that I am playing hard to get. Then again, perhaps I should be thinking that this is a man with a keen sense of something and I should respect that and give him at least a chance. But, I do not like him. My instinct isn't giving me hard specifics, but I feel an undeniable pang of rejection for this man. I honestly cannot put a name to the reason for my need to extricate myself even from his gaze. Adam creates a gut-wrenching case of the willies in me so strong there are times I am sure that if he even tries to touch me I would surely become violently ill.

I am not completely without sensitivity for this situation. I know what the man wants. I know what my family expects of me. I also know what I want, in life, and in love. I think that as human beings we need to grow and become more than we were. To want to be more, do more, think more and love more is a goal that I expect myself to achieve every day. I want to develop and nurture the kind of relationship that goes far beyond attraction or chemistry and becomes the kind of partnership that makes legends. They say that you are either in lust or in love. I want love. Enjoying life with someone I love, who loves me as well, would be the perfect life in my opinion. Loving a man just because he is acceptable in my family's estimation is not a priority for me but I am acutely aware that this is their expectation.

I do not think that I can love Adam but I cannot bring myself to tell him that he is unwanted.

The better the day, the better the deed.

"Mr. Campbell, please."

"This is Mr. Campbell."

"Ah! Yes, Adam, I understand that you have established quite an interest in my daughter."

"Yes, Ma'am. I am quite taken with her." He was genuinely impressed by this aggressively proactive move by such a powerful and respected matriarch.

"You understand that I must insist that you treat her with the utmost discretion, Adam."

"I wouldn't have her any other way . . ." Adam's voice trailed off as though the impending silence implied a volume of questions.

"Perhaps we should meet for lunch and discuss certain matters. Are you free to meet me at The Vineyard tomorrow?"

"It would be my distinct pleasure, Ma'am."

And so, the task was set.

The luncheon between Mother and Adam Campbell came and went with two successful and accomplished people seemingly having the most innocent of lavish but tasteful meals. The very end of the conversation would not have been considered to function on any acceptably normal level, I should think.

"My daughter is a willful child and always has been. She has some very interesting ideas about how one should live life." Mother seems to slight me at every opportunity with a most distinctive pleasure even when I am not there. "She is an excellent prospect for a man of your caliber and while the only woman worth having is one who can be properly trained, I think we might agree that the challenge of her misguided willfulness entices you even more. Yes?"

Adam's recognition was controlled but palpable. "Agreed."

"Sometimes the subjugation of a woman must be achieved by any means."

"Surely you are not suggesting that I take your own beloved daughter in hand by means of any kind of subversive action."

Mother responded with a brilliantly delicate smile. "Some believe that a life-altering experience which is shared can create an unshakeable bond. Whether that is good or bad is immaterial."

"The experience, or the bond?" Adam was on the edge of his seat visibly shaken, amused and curious.

Her only response was to smile and sip her tea.

Life isn't fair. It's fare.

September has arrived and thus, a new semester at law school. I have managed to arrive safely to my final year. After this, it is just a matter of passing the bar. I have already spent the past six years wowing the firm of my dreams so I am assured of a position however junior and perfunctory. It is a top-notch place to be with impressively grand names and an illustrious history so I am hoping that this will be the final straw and a little love from Mother will be forthcoming. I live in a dream world, but it's mine.

Adam is still a pest and Madison is still the light of my life. The separation from him will be welcome but missing her will mercilessly haunt my every day and night. She is three hundred miles away working on her thesis in astrophysics.

I can still feel her last touch when we said our farewells to summer and to each other's constant presence. We had agreed early in our relationship that work was work but certain vacations were to be selfishly spent on time as a couple and the arrangement seemed to achieve great results in keeping the love between us thriving.

It was as though an invisible cord connected our hands and hearts together and as we turned to go our separate ways, the cord resisted somewhat as if knowing that we could not bear to leave that space and time. United by hope and promise, the cord relented in faith and eased as it altered to accommodate our distance knowing that nothing could keep us far apart for very long.

Madison even smells divine. It seems only natural that she should be so conversant with the Universe and the ancient wisdom that makes this world. Her demeanor is rare and she exudes an unobtainable quality. People are drawn to her insight and wisdom and repelled by her unusual strength. She is warm and musky, with undertones of some resinous and revered wood that has stood the test of time in a hidden forest where only wild things exist.

On weekends when I cannot see her, I go hiking in the mountain forests just to feel her. I walk among the rocks and ravines and wonder what elemental forces formed the landscape. I try to remember the feel of the power of her body against mine when last she bent me to her will like a force of nature and the memory renews the architecture of my soul.

I stay long enough to watch the stars pierce the impending darkness with the promise of the permanence of cycles as day gives way to night and I imagine that she is with me. She points out the movements of the constellations. She chuckles warmly when I can't decipher the difference between the bright ones and a man-made satellite. She holds me as I shiver against the enveloping damp and as proper reserve gives way to undeniable need we make love like the untamed for hours. Even if only in my mind we can share that moment, in that place, then in my mind I cherish the precious gem that is Madison Chambers. She is the brilliant and everlasting star that lights my path and the fire that protects, purifies and sustains every part of my being.

She is always reminding me to focus. "Be present every moment. That way, you won't miss the magic." She talks of illusion and science as if they are timeless and inseparable soul mates. I am sure she has read so much that it has melted her brain. Of course, she says the same thing about me. "Torts for tarts!" is her favorite phrase to tease me. It works.

But trying to focus on the present when all I can think of is the possibility of a future rendezvous or the memory of a long past liaison of lust and fulfillment drives me mad with desire. I can bear it for so long until I must go to find her and turn the aching potential to kinetic bliss. She makes me feel alive.

Sometimes she comes to find me.

It is the fifth weekend of the school year. There is a tree in the front of my window that has revealed its colors in the most brilliant hue of bright gold that I have ever seen in my such few years. Knowing that many more are to come, I am still not sure I can ever outshine this autumn. It has been raining for two days now and the nights are beginning to dawn to frost on the windowpanes. I wonder if the first flakes of snow will see any of these beauties, seemingly lit from within by the sun as the wind dances with them long into the night. The air's anticipation has become crisp with desire. The wise scent of time blooms radiantly knowing that it is indeed her turn to shine on this day for this moment. There is so much to learn.

Many of the undergraduates have been shamelessly begging to be initiated in the old and established ways of the wisdom of the heathens and the older students can barely mask their delight at the prospect of educating new flesh. I can barely mask a knowing giggle as I pass one of the fraternity houses on campus. The loud and driving beat of the hypnotic music winds around us like a dark and seductive gypsy's hedonistic call to the dance. The creative force of knowledge appropriately coupled with innocence is strong enough to make you acutely aware of its' tangible presence. There is a time and space where the rhythm of this kind of energy can take you places that dreams can only lead you. This was one of those times. There is innocuous drink and abandoned laughter and nubile, fresh bodies everywhere. School is in session.

Three hundred miles, and she appears like a hungry beast at the edge of the forest. It doesn't matter who is the hunter or who is the hunted. I grin from ear to ear all weekend long and thanks to the charmingly quaint bed and breakfast in the next village, no one is the wiser.

To be honest, I learn a few things myself.

There are places on a woman's body that by all of polite society are considered completely innocent. And yet, when touched in certain ways, you can achieve such a pleasurable result that for some, it can be considered even greater than what is known to be the more traditional forms of cause and effect for satisfying sex. Needless to say, Madison and I have found that the discovery of these places with each other to be beneficial for our relationship and delightfully rewarding. So much can be communicated by non-verbal means. The tilt of the head, the twinkle in an eye or the shiver resulting from such a touch can tell you more with unparalleled efficiency than any language can relate.

However, if there is one thing that I have

learned it is that we all must live in truth. We all have relative truths that are quite personal and they can also extend to the limits of the known universe, but we are all responsible for it. I would stake my reputation and life on the preservation of it. Without truth, we all fail. I think that is why I want to work with the law. We all have an inherent right to live in truth. I want to see that happen. It is time for humanity to grow.

In fairness, I do not know what it is that makes me gay. Oh, there are studies that claim this or that, painstakingly detailing the formation of our sexual identities or religious tenets which fear and manipulation keep us from any further investigation of our most intimate selves. And then there are the words unspoken yet ever-present in the eyes of your loved ones who, whether they wish to or not, simply do not understand. In ways, it is possible to learn from their ignorance. I have found it to be true that it is not healthy or productive to reject anything solely out of fear.

I have some very strict ideas about love and some more free than others. But I have come to this idea that one simply cannot choose whom to love. Love is a process, a pathway and a blessing not often found. When one finds such a treasure, it tends to lead to a feeling of true celebration. We could be talking about an appreciation of music, a favorite food or a cherished family heirloom. How much more is the value of the gem of a person's heart? This is love. This is where we understand that we must un-learn anything that is not of love. We can honor the fragility of our humanity and still face any adversity with strength and purpose. True humility is not a perverse notion that everything we are is substandard. I believe that a firm and reasoned commitment to the authenticity of our existence is the real path to God. In truth, we find love; in love, we find Divinity.

I found love in and with Madison and I am most blessed.

Love is a four-letter word.

We were sleeping in late, one lazy Sunday morning, in that bed and breakfast that had become our hideaway home in the mountains. Heavy snows had come the night before and everything was covered in a bright, new blanket of clarity.

"I have an appointment tomorrow."

"Oh?"

"I found a lump."

The silence was deafening. The longer I waited to say something the more wrong it seemed to reply at all. For me, there are no words to be spoken for certain moments. And, it seemed as though Madison had so many thoughts of her own running through her head that anything I could say if only to attempt to make things better would only seem coarse.

I rolled over in the bed and propped myself up on my elbows to look at her. Her eyes were so blue, and they glowed at that moment in the searing light of morning. Her hair glistened as the strawberry highlights caught the fiery glow. She has the kind of beauty that no art can reproduce. I used to wake up and anticipate the smile inside that would bubble up within, just to see those eyes looking back at me. I felt an indescribable excitement just to experience her presence each time that I did. The way she moved and talked was unique and powerful. She made me laugh, and think and let go. I realized right then and there just how precious she had become to me. I prayed immediately that God would spare her life. And, in that charity, spare mine as well.

I curled myself against her form so as to bind us together as one and somehow I managed to find words to say. "I love you, Baby. With all of my heart, and soul and body, I cherish you." We made love for the rest of the morning as if it were the first time as well as the last. I took special care to touch her everywhere she would let me.

Afterward, she looked into my eyes and held my gaze. My head automatically tilted which is a signal to all who know that I am about to cry. I did let the tears fall, as they were innocent and full of consideration. I knew that my days with Madison were numbered and I wanted to celebrate her presence every moment from that day forward. It wasn't a negative surrender to defeat by forfeit rather a instinct-driven knowledge of what was to come and how to make the best of that time with as much peace and as little negativity as possible. I still fought the notion of losing her daily with the ferocity of a tiger.

I could not have cared less. I should have cared more.

The sound shot out of the room like a thundercloud thick with chaos. It was as though Mount Olympus was host and spectator to something not seen in millennia. The scene was set to the tune of megalithic proportions. It was a family dinner. The family minister was invited and in attendance. There was what seemed to me an inordinate amount of flowers for such a gathering. Neighbors and church elders that I had not seen in years were in attendance. These were people who had watched me grow up. That is to say, they knew the "party line". Throughout supper, there were gentle questions that turned to lurid accusations. Sighs erupted and faces twisted as if there was still love in their hearts for me, but they were confused and torn as to their allegiance. Now, I know, they simply did not understand.

I was sitting at my mother's dining room table minding my own business when the good Reverend, seemingly smoking from the collar up, began to shout. But for the most part, the highlight of the evening was to find out that I was a failure as a daughter and a child of God, I couldn't have possibly been paying attention all those years in Church and what I was doing with Madison was an abomination and surely the work of the Devil.

I was being violated, in my childhood home, by the people that I was taught to trust and respect. These people had watched me grow, even helped me. They saw the mistakes, the trials and the inexhaustible commitment to getting things more than just right. They knew my heart. Now, because my heart chose someone different from what they believed to be the acceptable, I was being judged and shunned for no more than having what is a natural desire to love the person to whom I was attracted.

I responded by asking anyone to produce proof that God found me to be a failure. I had a contradictory passage from scripture for their every damning claim. I knew more than most of them about their own laws and could prove it.

"You taught me that God created humankind in love and found us to be favorable in His sight. Now if God made me, in His image, and declared that good then I'm not sure where your issues with my development into the person I am supposed to be hold merit. The Supreme Ruler of the Universe made my genetic code and laid a path for me. Who are you to question God? But you always taught me to go to the source. So, I suspect that if we were not created capable of proving ourselves according to God's standards, we would not have been created. And if the real matter is your own personal assessments that I haven't developed according to your standards, please explain to me how this affects my relationship to God."

And then, to make matters worse, someone quoted the worn-out joke, "God created Adam and Eve. Not Adam and Steve." The whole room erupted in self-righteous laughter.

I erupted with an uncontrollable rage, but bravely continued, "You need a woman and a man to make a baby. You do not need a man and a woman to make love. Furthermore, you do not need a man and a woman to make a family. Come to think of it, Pastor Lowe, do you even know where your own first three children are at the moment, let alone actively parent them?" The gasps turned to loud coughing and moans. "Old Covenant and New Covenant combined, by your own teaching, God orders us to love all the world which is His own creation. I am a creation of God as well as my parents. It is therefore your duty not only to say that you love me, you must act. For you to think in your mind that I am somehow anything less than you for any reason means that you have willfully usurped God's almighty power to rule. You have deemed that God, not me, has created something wrong. So, in reality, you are judging God." I asked the question, but I did not really wait for the answer, "God is infallible. Yes? Then to question God is patent blasphemy. By your own vows, and the breaking of them through your seething prejudice, you have actively chosen the damnation of your eternal soul!"

It was a precocious act, and I knew I was in a lot of trouble to say those things. Now I think of all the things I could have said, or how I could have said things in better ways. Nevertheless, I refuse to regret one word.

Eventually, the only one left was Mother.

"I think you should know what I was forced to endure this afternoon."

"Did it sound like anything like the past several hours? I have endured enough as well, Mother. I am your child. Remember?"

"Yes! You are my child and I have suffered every day since you were conceived for that. Did your Father ever carry any of the responsibility for you? I did everything I could have done as a parent for you. You had opportunities other children only dream of with the schools and the organizations and the community work. How did you turn out so badly when I gave you every reason to be a success? I am so ashamed of you, right now. I am ashamed of myself!"

I could not look her in the eye. It certainly was

not the first time I had heard those words but they still cut me deeply, every time.

"Well Mother, at least now we know that the most important thing about other people's personal lives is your opinion of them."

"You are not other people, you are my daughter! Furthermore, it is not my opinion; it is the word of God!"

"No Mother, it is your interpretation of the word of God."

"Well, thousands upon thousands of people agree with me!"

"If thousands upon thousands of people jump off of the Brooklyn bridge claiming that God told them to do it, are you going to feel that it is your responsibility to do it for God too on their word, or would you rather hear orders like that come directly from the Almighty?"

If there is one thing a parent cannot stand, it is hearing their own logic repeated back to them especially when it is not to their advantage in a situation such as this.

If only on principle, I knew that it would be months before I was invited to another family dinner. I was relieved. However, now I knew that Mother knew that I was indeed gay, and everyone else who should matter knew too.

I left my mother's home feeling pity for my elders and no need to return, really. I was on my own and I always had been. It was time for me to take my own place in this world with no fear or threat of rejection or sanction. For if I am to believe in anything that I was raised to believe, then I am the creation of an omniscient and loving God and that is all the validation I will ever need.

My only solace was that Madison was not there to witness this travesty. For once, I am glad she wasn't there. Tomorrow was going to be a big day and suddenly no one else mattered.

Honesty is always the best policy.

It is Monday, and eleven o'clock in the morning and I have not heard from Madison. It is early yet, and I admonish myself for worrying, but I cannot help it. I am not going to any classes today or doing any work. I cannot think past walking and breathing. I cannot help it. I wonder if this is how insanity begins. The relentless navigation of feelings, careening between hope and hopelessness forces me to focus solely on my survival of each minute. I feel as if there is a gun loaded with a single bullet pointed to my head as I watch the rest of the world pass idly by like a traveling circus.

There is a time in every person's life when they come to the conclusion that immortality is not an option. The lower the age that this happens, the more cynical they seem to become. It is as though all of the magic and wonder of innocence becomes nothing more than an illusory dream. The potentials and probabilities that one could make real fade away and are replaced by a raw resignation of accepting whatever may happen. The fight for freedom is over. The need for fulfillment and joy withers. The soul finds no solace in either familiar things or discoveries. The need to learn, or even grow, simply fades to an acceptance of an unchallenged pathway to destiny.

Suddenly, the phone rings like a tower bell on Sunday morning, calling all the faithful to attention. I see that it is Madison and answer with a firm attitude of hope.

"It's good. It's not as bad as I suspected. I won't go into the details because the battery on my headset is about to die, but its way better than I had even hoped."

"Baby! Tell me!"

"I will have to have a radical mastectomy on both sides. They can minimize the scarring with restorative surgeries over time. There will be chemo, too."

"But, we can fight this, right?"

"Well, I guess I finally get to be the Amazonian Queen I always wanted to be."

Her tentative laugh left me silent.

"I'm going to look like a freak!"

"You're going to look alive."

"Come on, Honey. I will have more scars than Mount Rushmore. The chemo could kill me, anyway. I am going to have to put a hold on my Doctorate. I still may never get to do all the things I have planned in life. Who came up with the idea of a damned bucket list, anyway? I want to hunt them down and hurt them! And, the biggest thing is that I am afraid to let you look at me, let alone touch me, ever again!"

"Why?"

"Because I will never be whole!"

"Whole."

"Yes! Whole!"

Have you ever known someone so wonderful that the respect, admiration and desire that you felt for them actually hurt? Madison's words cut through me like a whirlwind and I actually felt woozy for a moment. We didn't talk like this. We worked at animal rescue shelters and supported organizations that helped domestic violence victims. I learned how to drive a nail in one blow, building a house for one of her neighbors because they lost it in a tornado. We chose our prospective careers out of a desire to do good in the world. We talked too long some days about things other people do not even think about out of a belief that even one proactive action could make a difference for the future of all humankind. We cared. We planned. We acted on our convictions. The voice I was listening to now surely did not belong to the woman with which I found love. Her voice was being replaced by the voice of fear.

I had never raised my voice to Madison, ever before. However, something just welled up in me at the sound of her words that set my tongue on fire. Moreover, once I started, I could not stop. "Madison! I love you! I do not love your breasts! I love you because you make me laugh, and think and care enough to cry. You see things in ways that amaze me. You encourage me when no one else can, or wants to. You have won awards that most people cannot even understand what they are for. You challenge me in the most delightful ways because you are the only person I cannot argue with successfully. You give everything you have, everyday. You're respectable. You do good things with no thought of any goodness for yourself. And, you make my knees weak every time you even think in my direction. What about what we have already shared? Does all of that just disappear into thin air, because you are missing a functional part or two? I don't care if they whittle you down to nothing more than a spinal cord and two eyeballs! You are still you! Now, I am getting in my car, and I am driving to your apartment and we are going to talk. You have three hours to get ready. And mop your kitchen floor because the last time I was there it was so sticky from that model of the milky way, or whatever it was, dripped glue everywhere and I know you've been too busy to bother to clean it up!"

I bit my lip, waiting for a response. I could hear her car speed up, but then the phone went dead. The battery in her headset must have finally given way, or I was just dumped by my girlfriend.

~~~~~

I arrived right on time, which was amazing considering how long it took me to get my hair just right. I figured if it was the last time I was going to see her, I wanted to look as good as possible.

There was a police car sitting in the driveway, so I parked on the street. I chuckled to myself as I remembered Madison telling me that her new neighbors liked to drink, and fight, and make up on a regular and rather loud basis. I got out of the car and proceeded to walk up the stairs to the apartment only to see that her door was wide open and that was not normal. "Oh great." I thought, "They've pulled her into their drama and don't even realize she has enough of her own. Do other people ever think of anyone outside their own skin?"

Just then, a police officer exited the open door and began putting up a yellow banner around the balcony. I took three steps up the stairs when a man in a black suit barreled out of the door.

"You can't come in here, pending

investigation."

The look on my face must have elicited a sort of mercy in him because he met me at the bottom of the stairs.

"Where is Madison?"

"Did you know her?"

"You mean do." This was more a statement than a question.

"Who are you? Are you a family member?"

"I am her girlfriend."

He glared at me, narrowing his steely eyes and bit his lip. "Does Madison have any living relatives?"

"No."

"Do you know anyone who might want to kill her?

"Kill her. " I repeated the detective's words as I tried to process their meaning. "Madison is dead. Madison is dead? What? How!" I crumbled to my knees before him, hands clasped over my mouth and pleading with my eyes now blinded with tears. "Please, no! Please, no!"

"Ma'am, we have more questions than answers right now. But since you are the only person we can get any information from, I suppose you will have to do. What I will tell you now is in the strictest of confidence." He paused, waiting for a show of compliance.

I whispered, begging. "Please!"

"A few hours ago Ms. Chambers' car was found on the entrance ramp to Interstate 80, westbound, on fire as the result of a bomb. The body still needs to be identified, mind you."

"She was coming home from the doctor's office." I began to choke. I couldn't breathe. I wanted to call him a liar. I wanted to claw his eyes out. Why was he being so disrespectful to me? Why was he telling me anything, if I was not family? Why couldn't this be a dream and I wake up?

"Can I take you to the morgue? I need someone to identify the body."

With that, I began to scream.

There is life after life.

The sight of Madison's charred body has never left my mind's eye. I live with the terror every day and every night. I hear her voice sometimes, when I am cooking, or when I'm in class or just walking down the street. I stop and look in some sick hope that she will be there. All I see then are the remains of my lover laid out on a cold steel table like a scene out of a horror movie. It is not entertaining in real life. I doubt it is entertaining at all. I think people just dare themselves to watch because they believe it protects them from the tragedies of life. Nothing prepares you properly for the reality of death. I don't care how tough you think you are.

There is no joy for me. I find no solace or purpose in anything or anyone. I wish I had insisted on going to the doctor's appointment too, but I had that stupid dinner to attend at Mother's. What a travesty that was. I thought it was over the moment I left the house. Little did I know that losing my childhood network of cherished friends and valued mentors would mean nothing to me in less than the span of a day. I honestly want to die.

No one seems to understand, either. They all tell me to cheer up, or that it does not honor

Madison's memory to mourn her in the way that I am. They say that I am young. In time, I will get on with my life and forget her. Reverend Lowe pulled me aside one day and explained that it was God's will because we were living in sin.

Mother seems to think that all will be put right in my life and of course the prospect of my soul's salvation if I would simply finish school, find a man and marry. She mentioned Adam Campbell last time and so I am sure this is the man she has in mind to save me from eternal damnation.

~~~~~

My loneliness is palpable. I feel her all around me. I smell her sweet, warm musk in the air like a thick cloud, which can never be gathered and kept safe from evaporating. It passes through me like a ghost that never speaks, but is always there. Her memory haunts me. Every moment we shared together is ever-present, and painful. I will never see her again. I will never touch her skin. I will never feel the warmth of her embrace, taste her kiss or look into her ocean-blue eyes. I can dream, only to wake to the bitterness of cold sheets. My love is no longer alive and with her, the bulk of my soul is gone. I realize that there is no love in this world for me, anymore, and the gravity of this weighs on my chest like a ton of cold and piercing ice.

Surely, God did not want me to live like this. Surely, I have the right to be happy. Surely, there is mercy, even for me.

For everything, there is a season.

The knocking tore at me like a claw from a deep sleep that I didn't want to end. I grudgingly pulled back the sheets like a child on any given monday morning during the school year, mumbling and feeling extremely inconvenienced. The door seemed so far away, yet the insistent pounding was so loud I ran as quickly as I could to answer without hesitation, if only to make the noise stop. On the other side of the door stood my faithful friend and favorite study partner, Patrick.

He was smiling brightly and his voice sounded so cheerful. He presented me with flowers and waited for me to invite him into my apartment. I was confused. I didn't realize that he was expecting me at the library. I did not have the energy or inclination to find out, all the same. I had no choice but to let him in. I'm not certain that I had the strength to get rid of him, either.

"I'm sorry I'm late. I'll go get dressed."

"Do you know what time it is?"

"I don't even know what day it is."

His laugh was the kind that elicited response.

No one could extricate themselves from Patrick's expectations, and he always got exactly what he wanted, whatever the situation. There was little doubt in anyone's mind that he was going to make a very good lawyer as he seemingly never even had to argue a matter, point or case. "Take a shower first. And put some make-up on that sun-deprived excuse for a face. We are going out."

"Why? Aren't we reviewing the murder trial for Professor Langley?"

"No. It's Saturday night and you haven't seen the rest of the town in several months now. There is life beyond campus, my dear."

"I am in no mood."

"Get in one, then." He looked at me, half with concern and half with a look of wistful hunger for a party. He had no qualms with making me think that I would be doing him a favor by going out with him so that he could have some fun. "Finals are in three weeks. I think it is time to walk on the wild side for just one measly night before we have to buckle down and really study. Deal?"

I giggled. I knew what he was doing, but a pint at our favorite gathering place would make him happy and get him to leave me alone. I knew there would be others there. I could rid myself of a searing headache and hand him off to some other friends before he discovered my absence. He would be lost in the laughter and music long before he noticed I had slipped away. I could make him happy for his charity in saving me from yet another lonely night. That was his mission. He was a good friend and he really did care. There was no sense in fighting him; this was his good deed for the day. I went into the bedroom without argument and began preparations. If he was surprised, he did not show it.

~~~~~

I stepped into the living room wearing four-inch Italian leather pumps, blue denim jeans that one does not breathe out to zip into and a blouse with far too many buttons left undone.

"Now, that's what I'm talking about!"

"Is the black eyeliner too much?"

He winked and motioned toward the door. "Let's get out of here before we don't."

The streets were buzzing with traffic. The entire town seemed to be alive with an electric hum. The music from the pub could be heard from a block away and there were hoards of happy people flirting and dancing on the sidewalks and in the gated courtyard. It promised to be a rather good night.

We didn't take three steps in the door before there was a communal shout directed our way. I laughed tentatively but instinctively walked over to our usual tables in the corner and began the usual greetings and salutations. I saw most of these people everyday on campus but there was something different about being in a social setting with no books for props or protection.

"Where have you been?" Some of the girls chided me as if I were some wayward soul who had lost my way.

I rolled my eyes and looked around as if I were looking for myself. "I was here just a minute ago. I know, I just saw me!"

That got everyone back to the laughter and the chatter. I was safe for the moment. Patrick disappeared and reappeared quickly with a frosty mug of beer in both hands. He disappeared just as effortlessly when he saw his latest beau walk through the front door. I realized that I was safe from a full night thanks to that guy and home free, too, as soon as I could down my beverage without causing too much notice. I made a mental note to pay more attention to Patrick's love life and ensure it would always progress well, if only for sinfully selfish reasons.

Too many beers and a few shots later I found myself unable to stop talking, even on the dance floor. I had completely forgotten my devious plan to escape the unwelcome chore of socializing with my compatriots. Everyone seemed so merry. Every song playing on the jukebox was someone's favorite. We sang loudly, danced wildly and toasted each other with grandiose ramblings. We talked about things to come and of exploits that made us look as innocent and ignorant of the real world as we really were. We were the future benefactors of the entire universe and we were damned proud of ourselves, too.

It was the last dance of the night. I recognized this because at Mardi's the tradition was to play a slow song. I suppose it started as a way to make the last call for drinks without screaming over the patrons, but people seemed to love the idea of one last chance for a promissory kiss and cuddle with whomever one hoped to be spending the remainder of the night. In every college town in America, I imagine the prospect of being seen going home alone brings out the best players at catch-as-catch-can.

I began to walk back to my seat as I was a single girl now when someone grabbed my arm. I wheeled around quickly and too far as my high heels coupled with drunkenness betrayed my sense of balance. There, standing against me so as to keep me on my feet, was none other than Adam. He was grinning from ear to ear and so was I.

Tough love is kind, not blind.

I awakened to the sound of birds singing sweetly on my windowsill. The sun was streaming through the open curtains and searing right into my brain. Everything hurt. No sooner than I had brushed my teeth, which was assuredly an action of personal honor, the phone rang.

"Get your lily white out of bed and fire up the cappuccino maker. I'm leaving La Mode now."

"Deal!" I loved the way Patrick thought. He knew how to take care of the details and this morning I certainly could not play the devil even if I felt as though I had danced with him all night.

Fifteen minutes later, I was barefoot but clothed and my hair was in a ponytail as I stood in my kitchen, attempting to make an acceptable froth. The doorbell rang and I opened the door quickly and wide without looking through the peephole. Standing at my doorway, Patrick and Adam stood, looking warily at each other and then me.

"Call me the cat." Patrick stepped over the threshold and into the kitchen without waiting for an invitation.

Adam stayed at the door with a fragrant and lovely bouquet of lilacs in his hand. "I see you already have plans for the morning but if I could tempt you, what would you say to dinner and a movie tonight?"

"The remainder of her weekend is completely booked. My apologies." With that said Patrick reappeared in the entryway, took the flowers out of Adam's hand and promptly slammed the door.

"Hey!"

"Would you have accepted?"

"No."

"Then, no worries. I brought you a butter croissant for now and a tart for later. Darling, you seriously need to learn how to make a proper froth."

I toddled behind him like a dutiful but needy child. "I'm famished."

"I'm concerned."

"About?"

Patrick pulled the pastries from the box and laid them on napkins as he sighed heavily and clucked like a mother hen in my direction. "Do you remember anything about last night?"

"We danced."

"You also kissed him."

I gasped, and my head started pounding with more fury than I felt for those birds at my window.

"Everyone saw."

I wanted to throw up. I gulped my cappuccino quickly instead.

Patrick half-laughed, half-sneered. "There's that look again. Every time someone even mentions Adam Campbell it looks like you vomit in your mouth and swallow."

I slumped over my cup and held my head in my hands.

"The official story throughout the entire community is that you were drunk out of your mind. You may thank me when you are able. Now, eat."

If there are no questions, then there are no answers.

I have begun to develop some ideas about the human condition and the permanence of life. There is no happily ever after unless we create it. I believe that the drive to create a family is more than instinct, rather a need to prove that we have the capacity for sharing our love. We engender community through authenticity and consideration. We make a family out of the belief that we have more than talent or wisdom to nurture another soul.

I want a baby. I am young but educated. I will be able to support the child as I have made a responsible career choice and have reliable prospects for the future. I am focused and energetic. I have a wonderful network of friends. If I wait until I am firmly established in my work, my lifestyle may not leave room for a child. But if I build the foundation of my tomorrows now with a child already rooted in the architecture I just may succeed at being a parent. It will be hard work; I have no doubt. I may have to rely on a little luck too, just like everyone else. But I believe that motherhood is always challenged by difficulties and perhaps it would be wise to just do it now instead of waiting for the possibility of an obvious and fail-proof opportunity.

I am gay. Society does not support a gay's right to family, or much of anything, really. If we want something, we are forced to make it ourselves or live without. It isn't right, but that is the gravity of our world's truth.

Everywhere I go I see children. Several of my friends have already begun to make their families. I desire, even need, to take my own rightful place in the making of my personal nest. I believe that one or two babies would fill it nicely. There would be laughter, learning, and memories to make a living legend of tangible history.

However, the serious matter of whom I might choose to father my children gives me pause for concern. There are genetic inheritance issues as well as whether or not he would take an active, or any, part in their lives. There are a variety of choices I can make, but I think I have come to my own ideas out of reasoned decisions.

I want to do this on my own. Quite frankly, I cannot imagine parenting a child with anyone other than Madison. We were so well suited. Now that she is gone, I find no one else attractive to me as a partner and mate. Surprisingly, I hope that this seemingly ever-present situation changes. I do think that it is possible for me to find a good love once again.

I just do not want to wait indefinitely until I find her to make a family.

There is the option of modern science. I could study the demographics of an entire population of prospects within the framework of a sperm bank database. I could choose every desirable trait conceivable for a child from eye color to favorite music. I could map out a congenital pattern by rejecting anyone who didn't match my criteria and considering anyone who did match. I could examine probabilities and possibilities of any number of quantifiable categories and substrata. I could make histograms and diagrams and I could make myself crazy, too. But can I, in good faith, fall in love with a man on an intimate level for his goodness as a father without actually loving him intimately like a husband when it goes against personal preference and principle? Science seems much less intrusive and much more accommodating, even with all of the physical trials and psychological tests I will be forced to endure just to prove myself worthy of doing what any straight person can do without anything more than a selfish desire to satisfy a moment of lust, ability to parent notwithstanding. Why anyone would actually choose to be gay considering all of the challenges, not to mention the matter of personal safety, is completely beyond my comprehension.

If every action considered is maintained within the framework of goodness, then the soul is free to wander wherever it may.

"Hello."

"Adam?"

"What a pleasant surprise. It is good to hear your voice."

"I wanted to apologize for the last time that we saw each other."

"Why? You did nothing wrong."

"I could have reopened the door, or replied or said something."

"You're saying something now." His voice lilted as if he were genuinely happy. There seemed to be no anger in his words. Admittedly, I was relieved. "So does this mean I get a second chance? I would be very honored if you would go out with me on a date."

I could only respond with a shy laugh.

"Are you free tonight?"

"Seven."

"I will hold you to this, you know."

"I will see you at seven, then." With that, I ended the call and tried to breathe as normally as possible. I wonder if my voice sounded like I was in control of my emotions, or if it was shaking as badly as the rest of me. I felt so guilty about the way I had treated Adam over the years. He had never done anything to raise concern, I had treated him badly and I wanted to make up for my rude transgressions. I rarely rejected people for nothing more than a feeling. Perhaps I had lost my mind, too, but I was trying to be nice.

~~~~~

"Have you ever been to Bob Mason's Steakhouse? They have the best aged angus in town." He looked at me out of the corner of his eye as he maneuvered his Mercedes out of campus and safe from prying eyes in the twilight. He was wearing a dark blue suit with a bright red tie that made him look like his mission was another corporate merger, not a casual night out on the town with a college girl. Perhaps this was his way of making an impression.

I was wearing a simple white linen peasant dress and I felt out of place. I realized that I would not be underdressed for a steakhouse, so that worry quickly stopped altogether. Then, I just began silently fretting over things like proper topics for supper and whether or not we would actually go to a movie. I resolved that I would not speak at all about the fact that I had rejected his advances, or apologize for any of my behavior over the years. I could not look weak or indecisive now that not only was I actually out on a date with Adam, but I had made the first move.

We began to talk and tell jokes. We reminisced about common hometown memories and gossiped about current events. We talked about the weather even though we did not have to out of a need to keep the conversation going. There was easy laughter between us and I began to wonder just what had given me cause for not liking this man for so long. He wasn't bad looking, in fact he might be considered handsome. He had good social skills, was slightly famous for his work and he knew more about things than I had dared to imagine. I found myself liking him. I decided that I wanted to be his friend and not just an acquaintance. However, I also resolved that friendship would be as far as it could go between us. He was far too old for me as there was nine years difference in our ages and life experience. We found a lot to talk about considering this gap. Nevertheless, I imagined this would be an acceptable excuse for not dating when the suggestion came. I knew it would come up. Adam was adept at asking for what he wanted from me without being aggressive as his manners were impeccable and I had given him far too many lessons in learning how many ways that I could say no.

We closed the restaurant. The staff stood watching us for probably the entire last hour of business as they had to stay and we were the only customers left in the entire establishment. As they were gracious to us, I trust that Adam tipped them well. Judging by the look on our server's face as we left, I think he took rather good care of them for their hospitality.

As we drove home, a sinking feeling tried to engulf me more than once. Then he would make another cautious, yet amiable comment and all would seem well inside of me yet again. I felt guilty for so many reasons, some of which didn't have anything to do with him at all.

~~~~~

"Let me in."

"Adam, you're on my couch. You are in." I looked at him with an incredulous look of surprise.

"I mean, let me into your life."

I looked down at my hands, humbled and contrite. He was asking me for friendship. I hadn't even rehearsed my argument over age difference in hours and now the point was moot. I responded with a quiet voice. "Ok."

"Tell me about Madison." He nonchalantly put his arm over the back of the couch and pivoted his body to face me in an unobtrusive fashion, intent and ready to listen.

"I met her at summer camp before my junior year at high school. We were both 16, so driving cars and shopping at the mall were our favorite pastimes. Neither of these pursuits is available in places like camp, so we learned how to talk to each other and share activities like horseback riding and archery instead."

He smiled softly and nodded, encouraging me to continue.

"It was completely innocent between us until our freshman year at college. However, between hormones and the familiarity of a few years of knowing each other, I guess things just progressed naturally. I think I was attracted to her the very first second I saw her but it took a long time to work out any kind of relationship beyond friendship as there isn't a how-to book or an advice column for adolescent gays. We have to figure it out for ourselves, you know. Actually, some people don't get it right until they are much, much older."

He raised an eyebrow and tilted his head, warning me that he was about to make a point. "Getting it right early or later in life isn't just an issue for gays, you know."

"Fair enough, but I know that you know what I mean. Anyway, we just grew as a couple and by the time we finished our baccalaureates, it was a no-brainer. We were in love for life. She made the world a better place. She was extremely smart and kind. She would give her last dime to anyone who asked for any reason. She was gorgeous, too." I told Adam stories and anecdotes as I recounted the moments of fumbling discovery that turned to the enchanted bliss that I had spent with Madison for eight years. I talked in lofty tones and elevated degrees of a beloved and cultured admiration for Madison. "We laughed and argued and learned about everything together. When she died three months ago, I died too. My future plans and dreams are over. I have to figure everything out all over again. I know I still want to work in the law. I want to have a baby. But other than that, everything is a familiar and despised blur."

Motionless, with his head propped up against his hand, he waited to give me a chance to add anything more. He was letting me talk. I did not get that opportunity much as a child, so when the rare luxury of expressing my innermost thoughts and feelings is given to me, I can get rather passionate and verbose.

I looked out of the window as the birds began to sing and realized that I had talked the entire night. "Oh, my goodness! Why didn't you tell me to shut up hours ago?"

Adam's laugh warmed my sorrow-worn heart. He did not seem mad or inconvenienced. "Thank you for sharing yourself with me. I thought I knew so much about you. Tonight, I found that I have so much more to learn."

"It doesn't bother you that I'm gay?"

"The human soul is ageless, timeless and limitless. It has no gender. We fall in love and mate with souls, not bodies."

"Thanks for letting me ramble all night."

"Thank you for rambling. I have to be to work in an hour or so. I should probably try and get home, change and meet this day in record time." He stood up and walked to the door, as I followed, and turned to look me straight in the eye.

"I am so sorry!" I really was, too.

"Don't ever be sorry for anything as honorable as an authentic truth."

Just when you think it is time to blossom, you have already bloomed.

"What are you doing?" Adam called me almost every day now.

"Walking to the library. You?"

"When will school finally be over for you?"

"I'm done. I'm just doing some research for a case that I'm following."

Adam laughed, half out of surprise and half out of wonder. "Woman, you are as bad as me. You have already passed the bar, you're done with classes and you're knee deep in idle research? You should be frolicking on an island, half-naked and working on nothing more than a tan."

"I can't leave just yet."

"And, why not?"

"Well, there is the matter of a graduation ceremony, you know."

"Ah! Well yes, but after that, are you going to allow yourself a celebration?"

He was teasing me, but I liked it. "I might. The whole gang is supposed to meet at Mardi's after the ceremony."

"Darling, I'm not talking about getting messy with your mates at the local pub. I mean a proper vacation."

I had decided that my vacation days were over considering my vacation partner would not join me ever again. "What purpose would that serve?"

"Hey. You have achieved something most people do not. You deserve some time off. You have earned it. Don't even think you can argue with me on this one."

I sighed loudly for effect.

"I have a proposal for you. In three weeks time, I am going to Switzerland on business. While I slave away in three languages at a foreign boardroom table, you can hike the Alps. Try to tell me that doesn't interest you. Plus, you will be helping me as I don't like to go on long airplane flights alone." He said no more as a way to force me to answer if only to break the tension in the silence.

"Damn it, Adam!"

Adam gasped, "Did you just cuss? You? My

ears have turned a pale shade of crimson, I do declare!"

"Your Scarlett O'Hara is frightful, you know."

"Get your passport ready."

"And what if my answer is no?"

"You would say no to hiking? You could walk for days and have only cows and birds for conversation, save the little hostels along the way. All that I ask is that you give me your itinerary for safety's sake. We will part at the airport when we arrive in Zurich and meet back there before we leave. I will throw in a first class ticket and a really nice rucksack. Now, what do you say?"

"I say you might be an accomplished negotiator someday."

"You are shameless."

"And?"

"You're going, and you're going to like it."

~~~~~

Everything here is breathtakingly gorgeous. The grass is a pure and virile green, the water is the most resonant of all blues and the crisp white of the edelweiss carpets the ground as if to memorialize the snows of the past. The air sings as it envelops your being, and the life force within it surely can cure the deepest of wounds. All that haunts you becomes nothing more than a long-forgotten nightmare. In the Alps one becomes a child again, full of magic, wonder and delight. There is a power here that, if you will allow it, will preserve the honor inside of you. There is no time, only the ancient wisdom of days that turn into night and seasons that always return. Surely, the secret of a soul's renewal is kept within the rocks of Switzerland.

"Oh, Adam! It was beautiful! Everywhere there is simplicity and purity. The people are so warm, they laugh easily and their English is perfect!"

Adam chuckled and exclaimed, "Darling, only Americans are so arrogant as to think that they need to know only one language. And the cows?" He teased me with unbridled glee as I regaled him with the tales of my alpine trekking experience.

"The cows all have bells that are different sizes, so they ring with different tones. This way, the farmers know which ones are where by their sound. And the food! I had this cheese that turns brown because of the way that they age it. It is very nutty and sharp."

"How did you get along trying to explain that

you don't eat meat?"

"Most places, they would make me shredded potatoes, like hash browns, but they are fresh. And they crack an egg into it and smother it with cheese. It was absolutely yummy and quite filling. I loved it!" I really did. I am sure I replaced every pound I might have lost from all the walking. "The sun was so bright, my cheeks and arms would burn every day. Every morning, I was white, all over again. I can never get a proper tan, anywhere." I rolled my eyes for effect and he seemed amused. "The houses are spectacular! They are constructed with this thick and dark brown wood, but not painted, as if they have been standing for millennia and will last for a thousand years more.

One day, I was walking down a well-worn lane and there was this old woman who met me at her garden gate. She honestly looked as though she was expecting me. She took me into her house and talked to me as if we had known each other forever. She had made these wafer-like cookies and we drank a delicious type of coffee with them. Her linens her exquisite, and finely fashioned with these delicate designs. The table looked hand-made and the wood was heavy and solid. The whole place had a warm and classic styling that I liked very much. I had to keep reminding myself that I was a stranger because I felt so comfortable there, as if I belonged and wanted to stay forever. She asked me the oddest thing. It bothers me a bit."

"What was that?"

"She said, 'Must one experience the truth in order to know the truth?', and I was so taken with her question that my reaction made her laugh. Her voice still rings in my ear. I wonder, was she asking me personally or was this some thread of thought she wanted to share? Was she able to see me, inside, and simply wanted to point me in the proper direction towards enlightenment? Was she lost in some sort of reverie and not talking to me specifically at all?"

"How old was she?"

"It is hard to say. These people are hearty and strong. It is deceiving, because they all look so healthy. They all look young."

"Perhaps you found the wise-woman of the village. Perhaps she was demented or senile. You're lucky she didn't poison you and cook you for supper."

"Adam, it wasn't like that at all. Do you think it is possible to find a family in people who aren't actually related to you?"

"I think that you should have been more careful. Not everyone in this world is good, you know. You are important to me and I want you to be around for a very long time."

"Why?"

"Oh, hell."

I swatted him on the arm and put on my best southern drawl, "I do declare!"

He pushed me back against my seat, and leaned over me as he unbuckled my seat belt. "The seatbelt sign turned off over an hour ago. But I love to hear your stories, so I didn't want to interrupt you."

Breathless from being taken by surprise, I replied, "You are a mean and selfish man. But, you have good taste." I could tease, too.

"If I were selfish I would have insisted on having you all to myself every night at my hotel this week which, for the record, was quite luxurious compared to a hostel but I digress. Instead, I have to listen to how total strangers had the coveted blessing of your presence while I worked like a dog for people I don't really like. Nevertheless, I signed the deal of a lifetime, and you seem to have had the time of your life, so I won't complain. Do you realize that you're glowing?"

If I had a computer screen on my face, it would have registered several exclamation points, followed by a few question marks.

"Not that you aren't excruciatingly gorgeous at any other time, but I have to say that you are more of everything now that ever made you the angel I have grown to love."

"Grown?"

"Love."

"Adam."

He took my hand and caressed it as though it were so delicate that it might break. He didn't say another word and just sat there, holding my hand. I knew instinctively that he meant the kind of love that friends share so I wasn't in the least bit concerned by this sudden confession. Truth be told, over the past few months, I had come to this understanding of platonic love with him, too. It was easy and comfortable. I was humbled and grateful for his presence in my life. We both fell asleep, exhausted from the excitement and length of the journey.

There is a time and a place for everything, and sometimes, there is not.

We landed in New York in the middle of the night, exhausted but happy, and decided to find a hotel before driving the rest of the way home. With the insanity of the airport behind us, a good night's sleep and a hearty breakfast were the only requirements of the moment. We got a suite with two bedrooms that were connected by a great room with a fully stocked bar. I ripped open a bag of chips as Adam found the ice machine for the whiskey.

He returned in record time, it seemed. "You really do need to learn how to drink this neat. The ice distorts the taste."

"That is the point."

"Oh." He shook his head and chuckled at me as he poured two large drinks, one with ice. "I am going to try to get you drunk, and I admit it."

"Whatever for?"

"I have full intentions of taking every advantage available to me in life. I am certain that if I can work this opportunity properly, it will go down in history as one of the greatest achievements of my life."

My laughter was colored with a look of incredulous disbelief. "You have been brainwashed completely by the fantasy that corporate power can do anything if you would consider getting me drunk an achievement."

He shrugged his shoulders slightly, looked down at his Italian leather shoes and seemed to suppress a look I did not understand. "It won't take much."

"Oh no, you didn't!"

"You're a lightweight and you know it." He handed me a drink and sat down across from me as he began to sip his own. His head was down as he laid his glass down on the coffee table, but I could see him looking at me as if he were studying my every movement. He seemed to appreciate me. I would often catch him watching the way I walked, talked or even how I brushed my hair. There was a respectful admiration in his eyes. I was amazed how a man who I thought was just interested in me as a lover seemed to have come to some kind of appreciation for the friendship that grew between us. I now felt honored, safe and warm in the scope of his gaze.

"Fair enough. I do know it. Have you ever wondered how they figured out a way to make alcohol?"

"I imagine it was a complete accident. Things go bad. People didn't know to avoid rotten food or drink until they got sick. It just so happens that it takes copious amounts of this rot to make you sick."

"The way you think sometimes amazes me. But you're probably right."

"I am always right."

"You are arrogant."

"And?"

"Don't."

"Don't what?" He actually giggled.

"Don't use my own ways with words against me. It isn't fair." My voice lilted. I was having fun.

He brought over the bottle and poured two fresh drinks. "Darling, if life was always fair, I would have had my way with you years ago. We would be married with 2 kids, live in a huge house with a white picket fence and have a dog named Bob."

"Oh, really now!" I drank the whiskey far too fast that time and choked.

"Slow down, there, Princess!" He was mocking me, but I didn't care.

"Three!" I pushed the glass across the table as if to challenge him. I knew I could hold my own. "I haven't even started, yet."

"Yet, being the operative word." He poured me another, like a dutiful friend.

"Princess?" I suddenly remembered him saying the name, and as the meaning registered in my consciousness, I reacted as if it were the funniest thing I had ever heard. "Oh, please. Don't even go there."

"You should be a princess. Or at least be treated like one."

This brought on a thick and frenetic silence as I tipped the third drink to my now warm and tingling lips and sipped it slowly, thinking about my future prospects and my station in life. "I want to be a good mother and a good lawyer. But, aren't the daughters called 'Princess' and thus, the mothers are called 'Queen'?"

"I believe that could be true." He sat forward in his chair, rested his forearms on his thighs and looked at me very closely through his eyelashes with his head pointed down. He was studying me again, and I felt a little bit nervous.

"Stop."

"Stop what?" He sat back and raised his glass in a questioning wave before he took another sip.

"Whatever it is you are doing." I fidgeted in my seat. I knew exactly what he was doing, but I had spent the last few months convincing myself so well that Adam and I were genuinely friends and that he accepted my lifestyle choices. I did not want to feel this from him. He wanted me and I was confused because I was not completely sure anymore whether I wanted to reject his advances. It wasn't as though this was the first time I had felt this way. In the past few weeks, I had come to feel more than warmth for him. I chided myself that it was simply a lethal mix of hormones and the loss of Madison. I had not been touched in far too long and it was inevitable, perhaps even natural, that I would want to feel love again. But, a man? I fought with this notion. I did not want to be prejudiced, as I had come to know the pain of gender confusion all too intimately with Madison. Was Adam right? Do we fall in love with souls, not bodies? How could I possibly be falling in love with someone else, only six moths after the tragic death of someone I vowed to partner with for all of eternity? Between the whiskey and these issues, my mind began to reel helplessly.

He sat forward in his chair again, studying me. I would swear on my life he was reading my mind as he exclaimed, "You are in overdrive."

I could not respond with any words, only a furtive glance that turned into a shy stare like the prey that can no longer run from the hunter. Presence, purpose and potential were instantly communicated between us and there was nothing that either of us could do but to succumb to the destiny that was waiting. I wanted to scream but I couldn't.

He was over the coffee table and kneeling against my legs before I realized that he had stood up.

"No," I tried to speak. All I could seem to manage was a most nervous giggle, which shocked me to the core. Here I was the one who could argue a case against anything with the fervor of a great orator, completely incapable of maintaining my innocence against this man and I did not even want to anymore. I really wanted to scream. I could not manage more than a whimper.

With one fluid motion, he enveloped me in his arms and pressed his torso against my knees, forcing them open so that he could hold my whole body firmly against his. He gently raised my legs in order to wrap them around him. Chest to chest and chin to chin, he kissed me with a passion that made my bones feel as though they had been set on fire. His fingers clawed at my clothing as his lips fed on my skin. It was as though there was no time to breathe and yet this went on for what seemed to be hours. He pulled back my hair as he kissed and licked and sucked every inch of my neck and shoulders. "You taste as sweet as you are," he moaned as he spoke with his voice sultry and wanton with desire. I suddenly had no perception of where his body ended and mine began. We melted together into one being that night and as he took me, he made me his own, over and over again.

One must think.

"She has lost her mind!" Patrick was literally bellowing into the phone, as he paced across my living room floor. Back and forth, he began to wear a rutted pathway into my carpeting as I sat, motionless on the couch waiting for him to recognize that I was actually present and capable of hearing every word that he said. "She is gone! Blotto! Call the trash man, she is junked beyond repair! I'm telling you, I can talk no sense into this girl. I need backup. Now!" He was calling in the troops. There was going to be an intervention and there was nothing I could do to stop it.

Didn't he realize that I was altogether and painfully aware of my situation? "Patrick, please!" He could not hear my voice. He was on a mission and there was no stopping him until my salvation was complete.

"You need help and I am damned well going to save you if it's the last thing I do before they put me in the grave." He returned to the phone, "Get your asses over here before I send out a search party. This is an emergency rescue!" He shoved the phone back into his shirt pocket and turned to face me as though I were on the witness stand for murdering a saint. "Have you lost every ounce of grey matter in your head? What do you honestly think that you are doing, here? I cannot even begin to believe what you are telling me. You cannot be in love with Adam Campbell!" He waved his arms wildly and kept pacing the floor and for once, it was not for effect. The man was livid and raging without reserve.

Within minutes they began to burst in, one by one, wild-eyed and wary alike. There were hushed tones of questions and disbelief, taunts of rejection and remorse and audible cries of perceived pain as they descended upon my apartment as if it was Don Quixote Central. Surely, I had had been bamboozled. Adam had hypnotized me, or utilized neuro-linguistic programming to control my mind. There was talk of voodoo. One friend suggested that I was doing this to gain the acceptance of my mother, an ill-advised attempt at pleasing the family unit so that I could be accepted back into the fold. I was accused of not being authentic, literally lying to myself, in order to find the love that I craved. It was natural, of course, they decided. So many other gays live a lie to save themselves the pain of rejection, loneliness and even violence. It would be a classic reversal of truth for the sake of escaping the societal pressure to follow the mob.

I began to fight back with rationalization, "Madison was as masculine as any bio-male.

Perhaps I love Adam for his soul. Their bodies may be different, yes. But their attitudes and demeanor are quite similar. They both excel in aggression, dominance and such. They are both tops. Technically, they just have different legal genders!"

With that, the screaming began. I could not make them see any sense of what I believed to be true and I could not accept their arguments either. Eventually, I just sat back down and listened in resignation. They knew that I was not about to give in, and I knew that they were never going to accept my new choice in love. In the span of about a year, I had now lost three major support systems in my life. I understood the gravity of the fact that I felt no need for caution considering that I would be shifting from one group's grace to avoid the wrath of the other. In my mind, I was simply choosing a path and following it to potential happiness and fulfillment. I thought that my life had ended with Madison. Why couldn't they be happy that once again, I had found a reason to live?

It is possible to make a hero or a villain out of anyone. It is just a matter of how you look at the facts. Everything is about perception. The more you open your eyes, the more you see. The secret is to be able to observe without prejudice, and accept without exception.

Adam makes my heart happy. I honestly believed that when Madison died, I would never again know the pleasure of sharing my life and love with someone else. I had rejected Adam's advances for so long because I was genuinely dedicated to Madison. My love for her was true. Cheating on her was never an option. I would have never even considered Adam as a prospect because I couldn't see anyone other than Madison for my love and thus, there was no need for another prospect. There is nothing wrong with the way I acted or felt over the course of all these years in consideration to both of them. Love blinds you to everyone except the object of your desire. I see now that it was natural, the way that I felt for him. I was already dedicated to a relationship and accepting his advances would have been a betrayal of that bond. I had done the right thing. I simply did not understand that my gut reactions and feelings are a form of protection that the sub-conscious can utilize to save you from destruction and pain. I had acted appropriately the whole time.

My life is so different now. I moved to a larger apartment away from campus. I love to decorate, and I am pleased with the way I have made a home for myself. It is efficiently comfortable and welcoming, and it's close to my office. The firm of my dreams did keep me on and I am quite sure that in good time, with a lot of effort and several successful cases each year, I should be able to make partner in excellent time. The future looks bright.

Adam and I spend a lot of our free time together, these days. We have settled into a good and proactive partnership. At the office, there are the texts and emails and the occasional flowers that he sends. We communicate often and well with each other. We have supper together almost every night whether it is at a restaurant or we have the luxury of spending time alone at one of our residences. Adam has a lot of friends and business associates and his social obligations are just as important to him as his responsibilities with his company. How we look is important to him. One must always smile and be pleasant, and be dressed impeccably whether it is a casual event or a royal gala. He likes it when I cook. I am not sure that I am adequately adept at making meals but I do try to set a nice table and lay out the tastiest yet healthy fare that I can manage. He can be jealous of my time and does not like to share me with anyone except to "show me off", as he calls it. I think he likes to be alone so that we have the opportunity for intimacy in our conversations as well as other things. We do share a lot of things in common.

He is good-looking. Many of the women we encounter react to his manly physique and demeanor. I have to admit that I get jealous when they flirt with him, right in front of me too, and I have to take a moment to compose myself. I must trust him if we are to make a good partnership. I have read that you can make something happen if you believe it will happen. By focusing and directing our will, we create our truth. If I want Adam to be faithful to me, I must have faith in his sincerity and honor. There can be no fruitfulness gained by expecting the destruction of a harvest. There is no success if all that you can see is failure.

We talk a lot about politics and world affairs. He has many ideas and some of them I do agree with wholeheartedly. It bothers me somewhat that there does not seem to be time in his life for acting on those beliefs. He is very busy managing his company and creating a dynasty for the future, so I can see where anything outside the framework of his own personal plan for life might be beyond his consideration at this point. I do hope that as he matures and gains more experience in life, he will see the need for reaching out to the community in order to make more of the world a better place. It is not that he is selfish; he is just rather focused on success at this point.

I like belonging to him. He makes me feel secure. When he holds me, I feel as though the earth could melt away completely and somehow he would never let me fall.

His laugh is infectious. He teases me constantly and will use anything as an excuse to do so. He listens to me intently, if only for the reason to turn my own words against me just so he can get a reaction. So, of course, I have learned to do the same to him. I find it fun, even amusing, the ways in which we play. We giggle and tickle each other a lot. Touching and affection are very important to him and this could not please me more. I like to be touched and Adam knows exactly how to do it just right.

I think I just might be in love. Perhaps it really can happen more than once in a lifetime.

~~~~~

"Woman, every inch of your body is divine. Your breasts are small and perky. Your lips are full and red like wine. Your legs are long and lean. Your voice sounds like the sweetest song, every time that you make a sound. Your eyes are like limpid pools of the bluest water. Your heart is pure and innocent. I like everything about you. Darling, you turn me on!"

I giggled with delight every time Adam said something like that. He announced these things with such fervor that I did believe they were his true thoughts and feelings. It made me feel special. Everyone likes to feel special. "Is this entire place great, or what?" The feel of warm sunlight on your skin and clean, wet sand on your feet is a sumptuous delight. We were lucky enough to be able to get away for a weekend in the Florida Keys and I could not have been more happy wearing a new bikini and walking between sea and shore with a man who matched me in every way.

We both had recently achieved successful outcomes to rather involved issues at work and we decided that we had earned a little playtime. We were walking along the beach when I mused, "Life is good. We have each other, we have our careers and we have anything we want ahead of us. Let's choose wisely. I want to enjoy every minute of the rest of forever."

"With me?"

I stopped dead in my tracks and turned to face him. I attempted to hide the fact that his question left me excited and breathless, but I am sure that the look on my face hid nothing of the emotions that I was feeling inside. I tilted my head, smiled softly and simply answered, "Yes."

He picked me up, threw me over his shoulders and raced headlong into the surf. I screamed with glee and a little apprehension as our bodies hit the salty water and succumbed to the warmth that enveloped us as we sank deeper and deeper into the ocean and the life that waited for us on the other side of tomorrow.

For two amazing days, we lazed in the sun, danced in the moonlight and made love as though our only need was to bask in the glory that was our union.

With the dawning of each new day comes the warmth and light of life's potential.

Something is different inside my body. I have not felt right for a few weeks now. My breasts are tender. My hips feel weak. At times, I have no strength and at other times, I feel quite literally buoyant. I suspect that I am pregnant. I do not have morning sickness, but I feel a presence beyond what is me.

Adam has noticed a difference in my demeanor and has begun fretting over me but he has not asked me outright about the possibility of a baby. He takes care to know where I am at all times and pays special attention to things like my diet. He has also suggested that I move into his house. He presented me with a ring last week, and on bended knee, he asked me to spend the rest of my life in his heart and arms. I accepted his proposal. I want a traditional year's engagement because while it is quite obvious to me that things may progress much more quickly, or at least differently now given my situation, I think that we need to learn and grow more as a couple since we have been together for such a short period of time. I can live without a white wedding but I cannot live without a father for this child and our partnership must be solid.

On the other side of this coin, I have begun looking at other women but not men. Sometimes the attraction is quite strong and with others, I simply admire them. I am sure this is simply hormones coupled with the fear of making a commitment in marriage to Adam. My parents were not exactly successful and there is a slight part of me that is afraid to fail. Of course, I have no one to talk to about this now and it is beginning to drive me a little bit crazy. I believe that Adam has become aware of my feelings because he is constantly suggesting new friends for me. They are always straight women who are often married to his business partners or golfing buddies. I am so confused and I do not know what to do. First and foremost, I need to confirm whether or not I have a child to consider.

~~~~~

Pregnancy affects the mind just as much as the mind affects a pregnancy. Maintaining a balance between ecstasy and fear occupies my every thought now. My belly has grown to such a size that I am sure I will never see my feet ever again. I did not realize some of the things that women go through. My feet have swollen to such proportions that I can only wear bedroom slippers. My back feels like the bones are turning to jelly and it hurts constantly. I am losing control over my own body and even though I am quite aware that these days will eventually come to an end, I feel as though it will never be over. My attitude vacillates constantly between negative and positive, and I have decided that there are indeed times when being able to see from both sides of a situation is an accomplished art as well as a curse. No one actually knows any of this except for the baby. We are completely alone. It is quite obvious that Adam and I are not going to make a marriage work.

Truth be told, I cannot imagine sharing the parenting of this child with anyone other than Madison. I miss her presence in my life so very much. When I think in terms of the future, I still see her in the pictures and patterns of what could be. I find myself imagining her here, with our child, laughing and learning about the delights that family life can offer. I want to make these memories with her and no one else. I want her to have an influence in this baby's life, as her ethics and honor are parallel to my own. I see her with the baby in her arms, sharing gentle coos and bright smiles. I want her to hear the baby's first words. I want her to see the baby's first steps. I want to give her the life that was so brutally taken from her with all of the ups and downs and turnarounds that fulfill our potential as we grow together over the years. I want to give her the right to celebrate this life with the baby and me. That will never happen now and my heart is still broken. Have I filled the emptiness I experience everyday with Adam, just to save myself from feeling the true brunt of Madison's loss? Surely, I have acted out of the ache of needing to belong and to be loved and there is nothing wrong in such choices. Perhaps, I have made a mistake in thinking that I could replace the loss of love by moving on so quickly. I wonder if it is possible to love more than one person in a lifetime without feeling as though we have been untrue to everyone including ourselves.

Adam became so controlling and domineering that I had to distance myself from him in order to focus on this creative process and find some semblance of peace. Mother rests in the knowledge that I have proved, without the shadow of a doubt, that I am simply worthless. In her eyes, I can never make good now. My family is gone. My friends are gone. Madison is gone. I must prepare for my every minute of life to be filled with a child who will require each and every one of those minutes and I do not know what I am doing. In three weeks time, I will be responsible for the safety and survival of a helpless infant. To say that I am scared would be the understatement of the century and yet, I cannot wait for this new chapter in my life to begin. I feel empowered. I have read everything I can find about everything I need to know to prepare me for motherhood. I think I am ready. I also believe that I will learn more every day for the rest of my life and I will make mistakes.

~~~~~

Adam knocked on my door for the first time in weeks. He was so drunk; he could not stand up straight. Instinctively, I knew not to let him in but I had no idea that the purpose of his visit could be so heinous.

"I want you to have an abortion."

"Adam, I am in the final stage of my pregnancy. There is no such thing as an abortion in the third trimester. You are drunk. Go home."

"I do not want to be a father, and I do not want to have a baby with you!"

"I release you from any obligation. This baby is all mine. Go home and do not darken my doorstep, ever again."

"You tricked me. I'm not going to pay for this kid. I don't even know if it's mine!"

"Thank you."

"For what!"

I had surprised him completely. And, as I slammed the door in his face I said, "You just confirmed that I made the right decision in refusing to marry you." I locked the door, went to my bedroom and cried myself to sleep.

Lucky is as lucky does.

An icy rain began beating on the rooftop in a slow and steady rhythm sometime after I fell asleep. It was so comforting that it lulled me in and out of dreams and kept me from dwelling on my problems. I needed that after Adam's visit. How he could make such an unreasonable demand, I will never understand. If he did not want to be present or active in the child's life, I could accept that. I was not mad about it. Realistically, it would make our lives easier. When parents do not agree, the child suffers. No one can be pulled in two different directions without dealing with the threat of breaking. The questions of, "Who is my father?", and, "What is he like?" would be inevitable. Nevertheless, how can one miss what one has never had? I know personally that this is just a natural fact. I cannot remember the last time I saw my own father let alone needed him. I will know how to handle the pain of rejection when the time comes that this child discovers that when it comes to his father, he is unwanted.

I began to hear a rhythm that was not the rain. I was fully awake and lost in thought now, so I knew I wasn't dreaming or imagining this sound. I sat up in bed and listened more intently as a shadow appeared against the wall in the hallway. Adam squealed in pain as he bumped against my door. I had forgotten that he had his own key. Obviously, he had let himself in and our little conversation was not over.

"Listen, Bitch. You are not having my baby. I won't let you!" On the last word, he pointed at me, fell back and slid down the wall to the floor.

The smell of vomit wafted through the room as lightening illuminated every corner. I could see his rumpled clothing as it hung on his rumpled body. I had to deal with him. I resigned myself to this immediately and considered my options. I pivoted my body and swung my feet over the edge of the bed. I stared at him for what seemed a very long time before I spoke in hushed tones. It was at least four o'clock in the morning and I had neighbors on either side of two walls. It was only fair to be respectful of their need to sleep. The fact that I was being inconvenienced by a drunken maniac was immaterial. "Adam it is late and we cannot have a constructive conversation when you are in this state. Go home and I promise we will talk in the morning."

"It is morning now. See? I know that. You think I am drunk, but I know exactly what is going on. I am not stupid, either." He wiggled his finger at me as if to indict me for lascivious behavior. He was not slurring his words as much as before. Perhaps I should just let him talk it out and be done with this fiasco as quickly as possible.

I put my hands on my belly and that was a mistake.

"You are an evil temptress. Do you know that?"

I decided that the less I talked, the more quickly this would end.

"I'm not altogether sure if you aren't actually Satan." He looked at me with one eye, as if he was assessing this for fact. "If there is one thing I can't stand, it's a woman with a brain. You're cute and so very entertaining, but you don't do a damned thing I say and that really pisses me off. Look at you. You won't even argue with me when I want you to!"

"What do you want me to say?"

"I want you to go and get rid of that baby. Then, you are going to marry me and we will live happily ever after. You are my Princess, remember?" He was whining and morose as he reached into his jacket and produced a full bottle of rum. He tore off the seal, opened the bottle and offered it to me to drink as if this were some way of making a deal. When I sat motionless and unblinking in tacit refusal, he said, "Cheers. ", raised the alcohol to his lips and took the longest gulp that I am sure is humanly possible.

I just stared in disbelief and hoped he would pass out quickly.

"Where are your manners, Princess?" He clicked his tongue against his teeth and sighed heavily. "You are such a petulant and willful child. What am I going to do with you?" He replaced the cap to the bottle and set it down on the floor. Looking like a lion about to pounce, he crawled toward me on the bed.

In a protective move, I pulled up my feet and covered myself with the blanket. It might have looked silly, but the idea of him touching me or getting any closer scared me witless.

"You think that blanket is going to save you?" He laughed in a way that I had never heard before.

I knew at that moment that I was in trouble. This would not turn out well.

"Is that your lucky blanket, Princess? Lucky, lucky girl. You have a blanket to protect you, don't you." He laughed tauntingly and stood up, weaving like a broken ring of smoke. He reached into his pocket and pulled out a gun, held it up at eye level and inspected it closely.

I gasped, which was another mistake.

"What?" He bent over me and looked into my eyes as if to say that if I would not speak, he would discover my thoughts and intentions in any way that he could. "You think you're smart, don't you. You think you can do whatever you want, whenever you want and there are no repercussions. You think you're special, don't you. You get the talent, the looks, the friends, the job, me, and whatever. Because you're lucky that way, aren't you. Well, Princess. Let's just see how really lucky you really are." He pulled out one bullet from his pocket. "Yes! Let's play a game and just see. Have you ever heard of Russian roulette, little girl?"

I had to speak then. "Adam, please!" My whole body began to shake and I whimpered loudly. Maybe it wasn't smart to show weakness, but any resolve I felt before was completely gone at that very moment. "Please don't do this!"

He began mocking me mercilessly with delight and waving the gun around in the air. "Adam please, what? Oh my God, I think you might be begging. Lucky girls don't have to beg, Darling. Didn't you know?" He put the bullet in the chamber. "Now, if you were a smart little girl, you would have done what I asked a very long time ago, wouldn't you. But no, you rely on the possibility that your cute little voice and your cute little face will win you some points and get you what you want, instead of doing what you're supposed to. So now, Daddy has to teach you a lesson. That's right. If you had just listened to me and done what I asked we wouldn't have to go through any of this sordid kind of business but it's in God's hands now because I can't help you anymore. You won't let me! So tell me, Princess, how lucky do you feel?"

"I am not a Princess and I am not lucky!" I shrieked as he moved to put the gun to my head, but he fell back onto the bed and then sat up quickly to regain control.

He continued mocking me. "I am not a Princess. I'm not lucky. I'm just begging for my life because I'm a selfish little bitch who wants to do whatever she pleases and come out smelling like a rose. Oh, right. Silly me!" He leaned forward and pointed the gun against the side of my forehead again as he began to explain the rules. "Now, there are six chances and only one bullet so you have five opportunities to live. Do you understand?"

The instinct for survival is amazing. You can lie, cheat and steal like a criminal if such actions will allow you to spare your or your child's life. "Adam please, I promise I will get rid of the baby first thing tomorrow. Please do not do this. Please! Let's just lie down and get some rest. We can go to the doctor as soon as his office opens. Please!"

"You give in way too easily, don't you." He sneered and continued, "You always did, come to think of it. You live your life like an open book. You are such an easy to love, beautiful, little whore." He put the gun in his pocket and bent down to kiss me hard on the mouth. He grabbed my shoulders and slammed me down onto the pillows in such a rough way that it felt as though we were throwing me against solid rock. "And you are my little whore, aren't you. You know, I think I want you alive at least for a little while longer. Yes, whores are good for certain things." With that, he ripped off his jacket and crawled on top of me.

Anyone who tells you that you cannot be raped by someone you love is incapable of sentient thought.

~~~~~

I awakened hours later feeling angry, violated and weak. The sun was high in the sky and I imagined it must have been close to noon. My body hurt and my head was throbbing. The ice storm had stopped and the silence in the room, except for Adam's snoring, filled my heart with dread for what might happen in the moments to come. It was then that I felt a stinging sensation in my feet and hands. My arms were raised over my head and I could not lift them to bring them down. It seemed as though my hands and legs had been bound by something, but I couldn't raise them high enough to see what it was that was now cutting into my skin.

Every time that I moved, even slightly, I sensed a pricking sensation that caused a warm liquid to ooze down around my ankles and wrists. I realized rather quickly that what I was feeling was blood. I thought that if I could somehow shift my body, I would be able to see what was keeping me from moving. But the more I moved, the more whatever was cutting me worked its' way into my skin and the more excruciating the pain. I couldn't help but shriek at the realization that Adam had done more to me than I even knew.

My thoughts turned to the idea that I must save this baby at all costs. I wanted this child. I wanted to be a mother. I wanted to live a very long and very happy life.

That life would not include a lunatic who thought he could control things by any means possible, which I now knew included violence. How many other bad things had this man done? I felt like a fool. He certainly had not coerced me into a relationship with him but it dawned on me that he was indeed very controlling, nonetheless. At an instant I could see, point by point, where he had indeed taken command over me. He had exacted a categorical and complete dominance over every aspect of my life. It was so subtle and slow a process that I never felt any sort of concern. I honestly thought that I was in control and making appropriate adjustments to make an equitable place of honor in my heart and existence for him.

But the facts were now glaring at me and the truth smacked of a painful reprisal. He distracted me with the need for constant communication. He alienated me from my circle of friends and replaced them with people he could monitor. Any social encounters we had with other people were with his people. He made sure that, outside of work, my every activity was his domain. We did what he wanted, went where he wanted, we even ate what he wanted.

I had not actually planned to have a baby with Adam, but when I discovered that I was pregnant, I decided that it was a good thing and I was happy. I wanted to have a baby. I made that decision independent of him before we were involved in a relationship. Perhaps, that is why it was so easy for me to see myself raising this child without him. I could not remember if we ever talked with any seriousness about children. Since I don't remember any type of details, I feel certain that the planning of a family was never discussed. Truth be told, we never really discussed parenthood even after I discovered that I was going to have a child.

The value of life is immeasurable. Every life is

important. Everyone has something to add to this world and no one's existence should be taken for granted. There is no way to ascertain what my own child will accomplish in life. I believe that with unconditional love, proactive guidance and proper nurturing, every human being has the opportunity to have a positive impact on their world. My baby should be given the gift of a chance at that and even more. I am committed to making sure that this child is raised in a healthy and safe environment. I cannot believe that his own father threatens his future out of no more than a loss of control over the situation. Emotions have a keen power over the intellect, and can shadow our thinking to the degree of making pitiful mistakes.

There comes a time in every life when you mature to the point of one very serious decision. There are things, situations and people that you will allow and those you will not. Adam has proven himself unacceptable and he is no longer welcome or allowed. He is unwanted.

My body ached. I did not dare to move or shift in any way. I was beginning to shake and my breathing had become erratic. I had not felt the baby move since I woke up. I had to believe that Adam was so drunk that he was in a blackout last night and that when he awakened he would release me. There would be an argument and negotiations, I was sure.

But he wouldn't actually make me go to have an abortion. No one has the right to tell me whether I can or cannot have a baby. Furthermore, as soon as he walked out of the door, I would call the police.

He began to rustle at the sound of my cries of pain. "Well, there you are. Right where I left you. What a good little girl."

His intentions seem unchanged from that of last night. I was afraid to speak. I was afraid to move. I was afraid for my life and the life of my unborn child. "I am bleeding."

"It will stop eventually." He got out of bed and looked at me as if he were calculating the time for such an event. "Don't try to move. It will only make it worse." He picked up his jacket, pulled out the gun and inspected it.

I laid there helpless and worn, watching him and trying to figure out just what he was planning. I could not help myself. I knew it was probably not a good idea to let my mind wander and wonder at the possibilities when I needed to stay focused on reality. The fear of the unknown is more of a prison than four ironclad walls.

Adam left the room and it sounded like he went into the kitchen but I could not be certain what he was doing.

Suddenly, like a bolt of lightning, I could hear Madison's voice as though she was right there in the room with me. *"Yes, stay focused. Stay right here in the present. You will know what to do if you are conscious of every moment. Watch his eyes."*

He came back into the room, and sat down on the bed with something in his hand that I could not see. I wanted to scream but I was afraid to annoy him as this might set him into action and I needed to decipher his intentions. Yet, I could not wait. I had to somehow gain control of the situation. If I were physically capable of moving, I might have more freedom and even an opportunity to flee. "Adam, I need to go to the bathroom."

"No."

"Adam, please!"

"There she goes with the begging, again!" He began talking to the walls as though they could hear him. He was most definitely not thinking clearly.

I wondered if I could use this to my advantage. "If I have an accident, I will make a mess. You don't want that, do you?"

"Do I ever get what I want? Ever? Do you know how long I waited, just to get you to give me the time of day? Do you realize what I have had to do, just to get your attention? Do you realize why Madison is dead? There has not been a day go by that I have not had to watch what you do or who you do it with because I cannot trust you! You know, I think it is about time that you start doing what I say, when I say. And girlie, if this is what it takes to show you that you belong to me, then this is how it is going to be. You are mine. I call the shots. I say when you have a baby, and I say when you pee!" He began flailing his arms wildly as he ranted and I could see what he was carrying in his hands for the first time. He had, in fact, gone into the kitchen and brought in a knife from the carving block. It looked so long and dangerous out of its' natural place.

My stomach turned into knots of despair and humiliation. I was responsible for Madison's death! Adam had killed her to get her out of the way, and it was my fault. All of the questions of the reason why she was murdered were now answered. Things began to make sense. "What are you doing?" I reminded myself to stay present and not panic.

"What am I doing? What are you doing, should be the question. Of course, it doesn't matter because from now on I am telling you what you are doing."

I began to wonder if he was still drunk. "I cannot move."

"What a smart girl you are." He actually seemed to take pity on me and explained, "It is barbed wire. If you try to run, it will get worse, without any effort on my part. Handcuffs and duct tape are for sissies."

"And the knife?" There was no point in acting innocent. In the movies, the killer always tells the victim what to expect. Bragging seems to be a universal need with criminals. Surely, it has something to do with a low level of self-esteem. Of course, why would anyone with love in his or her heart become a criminal? Perhaps that is a rationalization, but I don't think so. It was time to patronize Adam's ego.

"The barbed wire is insurance. The knife will take care of the problem." He stopped talking.

My plan to get him to tell me what he was going to do was not working. My frustration began to build in direct proportion to my fear. If I was going to die, there was nothing I could do to prepare. There was no one who would mourn me. I suppose it wouldn't be important to say any goodbyes, but I did have business to attend to and loose ends to finish. Also, I thought about how I might never be found, not knowing the details of this operation that existed in his master plan. None of this really mattered. I just wanted my baby. I began to let myself imagine that if we died together, we would spend eternity together, and in some sick way I found myself feeling relieved. In the end, I was just scared to endure whatever physical pain was in store for us.

Where was his mind, I wondered. How far does one have to go down the rabbit hole before one loses touch with a sense of right and wrong? We are all born knowing pain. We all will avoid it, whenever possible. If we do not like to hurt, then we know to not cause the hurt. If we can hurt, other people can hurt. Therefore, other people do not want to hurt, either. If you are not supposed to hurt yourself, then you are not supposed to hurt others. This seems simple enough to me. Why other people cannot grasp this universal concept is beyond my comprehension or patience.

"Right now, the problem is that I have to go to the bathroom."

"That is the least of your worries. Do you want to know what the knife is for?"

Perhaps I had given up too soon. His ego did need a bit of stroking after all. "What is the knife for?"

"The baby."

"What do you mean?"

"Do you ever listen? What have I been saying since last night? It isn't as if I haven't been talking about this. This is not a surprise! From now on, you do what I say when I say it. And I say that in no uncertain terms are you having this baby! It dies today! Done." He was screaming now.

"Fine. We will go to the doctor's right now."

"Oh, hell no. I am not taking any chances. You could betray me. Everybody betrays me." He pushed the knife against the skin of my swollen and silent belly. "You are never going to betray me, ever again."

The rambling was getting worse. The blanket statements and the scatological meanderings of his verbiage, I had thought, were the direct result of his drunkenness. But there was no denying it anymore. The fact of the matter was that the father of my unborn child had gone completely and utterly insane. And that was that.

"Now, close your eyes, Princess. This will be just like gutting a deer."

www.ingramcontent.com/pod-product-compliance
Lightning Source LLC
Chambersburg PA
CBHW071339130626
46556CB00004B/1950